KB089768

성구成九의 시절인연時節因緣

Seong-gu's Relationships in his Precious Days

천 마리 종이학을 접듯, 시조를 짓다

Writing sijo poems, as if making a thousand paper cranes

성구成九의 시절인연時節因緣

2024년 9월 2일 초판 1쇄 인쇄
2024년 9월 12일 초판 1쇄 발행

지은이 | 임성구
펴낸이 | 孫貞順

펴낸곳 | 도서출판 작가
　　　　(03756) 서울 서대문구 북아현로6길 50
　　　　전화 | 02)365-8111~2 팩스 | 02)365-8110
　　　　이메일 | cultura@cultura.co.kr
　　　　홈페이지 | www.cultura.co.kr
　　　　등록번호 | 제13-630호(2000. 2. 9.)

편집 | 손희 김치성 설재원
디자인 | 오경은 이동홍
마케팅 | 박영민
관리 | 이용승

ISBN 979-11-90566-99-5   03810

값 12,000원

K-Poem 005

성구成九의 시절인연時節因緣
Seong-gu's Relationships in his Precious Days

임성구 시조집 Sijo Poems by Lim Seong-gu

번역·우형숙 Translated by Woo Hyeong-sook

작가

시인의 말

한 생은 비록 미약했지만 절절한 희망으로 건너왔고,
또 창대한 미래를 위해 간절함으로 건너가는 중이다.

"처음은 미약하였으나, 끝은 창대하리라."라는 이 말을
심장 깊이 뿌리내리면서 가장 멋있게 살아가는 중이다.

'임성구林成九'라는 이름은
내 어머니와 아버지께서 피와 땀과 눈물로 어루만지며
푸른 숲(林)과 우주에서 큰 숫자(九)로 긴장하고 은유하며,
맑고 빛나게 이루(成)라고 내려주신 내 생애 최고의 선물이다.

그리하여 나의 지금은,
한국의 정형시 시조를 무척 사랑하고 아끼면서
슬픔도 뜨겁게 쓰는 이런 호사好事를 누린다.

2024년 8월
임성구

Preface

My life, though weak, has been with desperate hope,
now I'm on my way to a great future with a sincere heart.

"The beginning was weak, but the end will be prosperous."
With the words in my mind, I'm living in the coolest way.

The name "Lim Seong-gu"is the best gift from my parents.
My mom and dad raised me with blood, sweat and tears,
hoping I'd achieve something clear and shiny with a cool head
and a warm heart for evergreen forests and the universe.

So now I live with sijo, the Korean poetry with a fixed form,
loving and cherishing the poems very much.
What a blessing! I can write about sadness with a warm heart.

August, 2024
Lim Seong-gu

Sijo Poems Vividly Living

David McCann

poet·translator·former professor of Harvard University

How can the human and natural worlds be separate and distinct while still so deeply intertwined? The poems in Lim Seong-gu's remarkable new collection bring together sky, trees, the rain and the sun, with feelings, perceptions, or memories into moments of clear connection between the speaker in the poem and the readers who follow.

One of this reader's favorites is "A Ceramic Pot with a Poem on It."

The words inscribed on the body
look subtle in the moonlight.

The pot survived in the hot kiln
with ardent love for the poem.

The brush marks, soothing the universe,
help the love grow on the pot.

The poem's words bring to this reader's mind's eye the image of a poem-inscribed piece of ceramic pottery from the Goryeo period, 918-1392. It seems to take its shape as a sort of predecessor to K-pop, only we have to call it K-Pot : elegantly balanced movement up through the arms and shoulders of the sturdy pot, into the deep glow of the moon-lit stage. The centuries-old ceramic piece is lifted up by the poem text, and carried into frozen motion by the performative heat of the kiln.

We will find so many other poems vividly 'living' in this book, printed on the pages, to be sure, but also waiting for us to pick them up and read them, to savor the images, gestures, the special moments, and then turn back and read them again as memories of friends and family, local neighborhood places, and of our own images of the natural world around us come so vividly to life.

What a joy, this gathering of Lim Seong-gu's sijo poems! I enjoy their flowering again, and again.

August, 2024
David McCann

생생하게 살아 있는 시조

데이빗 맥캔

(시인·번역가·前 하버드대학교 교수)

인간 세상과 자연계는 아주 깊이 서로 얽혀 있으면서도 어쩌면 그렇게 별개의 것으로 구분이 되어 있는 걸까요. 임성구 시인이 이번에 발간한 멋진 시조집 작품들은 하늘, 나무, 비, 태양 같은 것에 감정, 인식, 추억들이 결부되어 있습니다. 작품 속의 화자와 독자 사이에 또렷한 연결의 순간이 이루어지고 있는 것입니다.

이번 작품집에서 제 눈길을 끄는 작품 중 하나는 아래의 시조, 「詩를 업은 항아리」입니다.

네 몸에 새겨놓은
달빛 문장 은은하다

천길 불구덩이도
견뎌낸 애절한 사랑

온 우주 어르고 달랜 귀얄문
둥개둥개 업어 키운다

이 시조 작품에 표현된 낱말들을 보면 제 마음의 눈에는 고려시대(918년-1392년)의 도자기에 시 한 편이 새겨져 있는 장면이 떠오릅니다. 이 작품은 일종의 K-pop의 전신 같아서 우리는 그냥 그것을 K-pot으로 불러야겠습니다. 견고한 항아리의 팔과 어깨를 타고 흐르는 우아한 균형미가 마치, 환한 달빛의 은은한 무대에서 조명을 받고 있는 것 같습니다. 수백 년 된 도자기 한 점이 시詩 한 작품 때문에 발탁이 되어 꼼짝없이 불구덩이 가마 속으로 옮겨져 그 열기를 견뎌 낸 것입니다.

이 시조집에는 위의 작품 외에도 생생하게 살아 숨 쉬는 시조 작품들이 아주 많이 수록되어 있는데 우리가 읽고 감상해주기를 기다리고 있습니다. 각 작품의 이미지, 제스처, 특별한 순간들을 생각하며 거듭해서 읽고 음미해보세요. 그러면 친구, 가족, 인근 장소에 대한 특별한 추억들과 자연에 대한 여러 이미지들이 아주 또렷하게 생각날 것입니다.

임성구 시인의 이번 시조집 발간은 참으로 큰 기쁨을 주네요. 각 시조 작품들이 활짝 개화하는 모습을 거듭 즐겨봅니다.

2024년 8월
데이빗 맥캔

차례 Content

3부 Part 3

단풍이 물드는 자리에 바람과 별이 지나가고

Where Foliage Turns Golden, Brown, and Red, Winds and Stars Pass By

1부

목마른 그리움이 피어나는 꽃밭에서 천년을…

|

Part 1

A Thousand Years in a Flower Garden
Where Poignant Longings Bloom…

춘몽 春夢

배나무 첫 가지가 연애소설 읽는 밤

겨우내 머금은 패기를 밀어 올린다

부르르 몸 떠는 꽃가지 내 형용사도 까딱까딱

Springtime Fantasy

At night time we read love stories,
   the first branches of the pear tree

are pushing up some mettle
   that was cherished through the winter.

Fluttering, the blossom branches wave;
   adjectives pop up in my mind.

천주산의 봄

산에 솥이 끓고 있다
진달래 피는 삼월에는

하늘과 땅이 맺은 인연
달천동*에 와 닿아

꽃물 든 밥알들의 완창完唱에
바람 분 날도 환하다

* 달천동: 천주산에 있는 계곡 이름

18

Spring of Cheonju Mountain

The mountain looks like a boiling pot
in March when azalea blooms.

Heaven and Earth are related
to Dalcheondong* in the mountain.

Red-tinted, the flowers look like rice grains
singing brightly on windy days.

* Dalcheondong: the name of a valley in Cheonju Mountain

탱자꽃

사월 끝자락 탱자꽃이 손 내밀 무렵
옛 고향 울타리 너머 순이 보조개 순해 빠져
가슴속 아리던 그 가시에 멍들어도 좋았다

그녀도 하늘로 가고 고향도 사라진 뒤
지키지 못한 약속에 새들은 목이 쉬고
아직도 울타리 너머에는 그리움의 강이 산다

Hardy Orange Blossoms

By the time the blossoms sprouted
  at the end of April,
I ever peeped at Suni's dimples
  over the fence in my hometown.
I didn't mind if I ever got bruised
  by the thorns that hurt me.

But alas she went to heaven;
  my hometown has changed a lot.
Birds are losing their voices
  from my promise I've failed to keep.
Even so, there's a river of longing
  still flowing beyond the fence.

낙화주落花酒

벚꽃이 하얗게 쌓이는 사월에는
술잔이 그 사이를 벌처럼 넘나들어
설익은 입맞춤에도 봄밤이 깊고 깊다

강물 위로 던져 보던 부질없는 약속들
푸른 그리움 되어 가슴에 스며들면
지는 꽃 잔에 띄워서 또 한 잔 말이 없다

Wine with Fallen Petals

In April, cherry petals,
  fluttering white, are piling up.
For some drinks, I lift a glass
  like a bee among petals.
With the kiss in a clumsy manner,
  so deep is the spring night.

Oh the pledges, made in vain
  and thrown away to the river!
They have come to my mind
  in the disguise of blue longings.
Then I have one more drink in silence,
  with fallen petals in my glass.

붉은 유혹

화장이라곤 모르던 그녀에게 봄이 왔다

홍매화 핀 입술의 수액을 먹는 봄밤

맨살을 기어오르는 바람의 손이 뜨겁다

Red Temptation

Spring has come to my sweetie
  who never put on makeup.

One spring night I kiss her wet lips
  that resemble red plum blossoms.

Oh the wind creeping over my skin;
  I'm feeling it is hot.

청도清道

그곳에 가보면 달디단 그리움 있다

오래 담긴 조선 항아리 노을빛 감물 확 번져

투명한 마을 입구가 복사꽃같이 따뜻하다

Cheongdo County

When you happen to go there,
　something evokes a sweet longing.

Antique clay crocks are colored
　like the sunset or persimmons.

The entrance of the bright village
　looks nice and warm like peach blossoms.

허밍

오래 감춘 비밀의 말, 쇳물처럼 익는 시간
산댓잎 우는 소리 절간 문을 두드리며
천 년 전 타악기 소리로 내 발목을 잡는다

허공에 올려놓은 똬리 튼 물뱀자리
깊은 동굴 벽화처럼 음표 몇 그려놓고
꼭 다문 입술의 노래, 하르르 나비 난다

Humming

When secret words, long-hidden,
  are in full swing like molten steel,
crying reed leaves on the mountain
  knock at the door of the temple.
Temple gongs, a thousand years old,
  are pealing to hold me back.

I imagine a water snake
  coiled up high in the air.
And music notes are added there
  like a painting in a deep cave.
I'm humming with my tightly closed lips;
  Flap Flap Flap, butterflies fly.

벚꽃 편지

손바닥 마주 대고 나무가 된 두 사람

눈빛으로 말하고 심장으로 쓰는 약속

혀 짧은 겹꽃잎 사랑, 행간 서로 뜨겁다

Cherry Blossom Letter

With palms facing each other,
   two persons became a tree.

The two talk with their eyes,
   promising with their hearts.

Oh hot love between double petals;
   the two whisper with a lisp.

목단 항아리

달빛이 베란다 문을 슬쩍 열고 들어와서

문갑 위 종일 웅크린 그 여잘 비춘 보름날

새하얀 엉덩이에서 수천 도℃의 목단이 핀다

Peony Jar

The moonlight is streaming in
through the window of the veranda.

The full moon lightens the jar
crouching all day on the low cabinet.

Peonies bloom on the bright white jar
at thousands of degrees Celsius.

댓잎 피리

봄눈이 사각사각 내려앉는 뒤뜰에

바람이 문 댓잎 한 장 허공에 올립니다

네 눈빛, 낙숫물 음계 짚으면 신들린 잎이 웁니다

Bamboo Leaf Flute

One spring day, flurries of snow
  are falling in the backyard.

A bamboo leaf in the wind
  is picked up into the air.

When you gaze at water dripping,
  the leaf cries excitedly.

차향茶香에 녹다

연녹빛 순결로 핀, 꽃이여 흰 나비여

잔에 띄운 이 연서戀書는 절집의 풍경소리

간결한 첫 경험에 취해 자꾸 말을 걸고 싶다

Melting with the Aroma of Tea

Oh flowers, you're pure light green!
  Oh come on, white butterflies!

The words of love in the teacup
  are like wind-bells in a temple.

Attracted by it for the first time,
  I just want to keep talking.

러브체인

허공 난간에 매달린 가난한 진물들이

서로를 보듬은 채 푸르게 몸을 꼰다

녹아서 꽃이 되기까지 그 꽃이 지기까지

Chain of Love Flowers

Some thin branches are hanging
  from the railing high in the air.

Embracing each other,
  the green branches remain twisted,

till the sap melts to have flowers,
  till the flowers fade and fall.

아니 기쁩니까

나누는데 눈치 서로 볼 필요가 뭐 있겠습니까

차가운 내 손 위에 더운 네 손 얹어주듯

마음에 꽃 하나씩 올리며 아껴주고 안아주고

Aren't We Happy?

Why do we read each other's thoughts
  when we want to share something?

As if you put your warm hands
  on my cold hands to help me out,

let's cherish and embrace each other
  with a flower in each mind.

꽃이 오는 방식

사부작, 사부작
토닥토닥 은근하게

비밀처럼 간직해온
묵은 그늘 그 안쪽까지

무더기 내리시는 선물
내 마음의 우주 만 평

How Flowers Come

Leisurely and not quickly,
flowers come out; how praiseworthy!

They also bloom in the old shade
that I've kept like a secret.

Oh they are presents from heaven,
making my mind vast like space.

사랑이 오는 방식

말하지 않아도 서로 아는 눈빛처럼

가슴에 천만 볼트 전류를 흘리면서

웃음꽃 팡팡 피우며 건너오는 진한 마음

How Love Comes

We seem to know how love comes,
   though we don't talk about the way.

Ten million volts flow through two minds
   when love blossoms between the two.

With big smiles, the two persons feel
   that they're in love with each other.

봄의 독방

혼자 있는 아이의 집
그 살구나무 손가락 사이

분홍분홍 봄이 오는데
울음 먼저 와 있습니다

애가 타 노래 들려주던 새
삭정아비처럼 부러집니다

Home Alone One Spring Day

A child is alone at home,
where there is an apricot tree.

Pink spring blossoms on the tree;
however, he's teary-eyed.

In a fret, a bird once sang for him.
But now it's gone like his weak dad.

환한 고립

덤불덤불 긁힌 자국 자갈 지나 찔레밭이다
엄마를 더듬다가 벙글며 벙글면서
하얗게 오월을 울리는 내 그리움의 가슴아

석 달 열흘 퍼붓던 빗물로도 다 못 채운
공병 같은 가슴아 공술 같은 노래야
어느 집 헛제삿밥 같은 이 허기진 그리움아

Bright Isolation

Rocks with bushes are in my path;
  a thorny path lies ahead, though.
Remembering my mother,
  I put a smile on my face.
Oh longing in my heart for Mom,
  when May comes, I'm tearful.

Even if it rains a lot
  for three months and ten days,
it won't fill my emptiness.
  Oh empty heart and empty song!
Longing is like rice piled up in a bowl;
  in spite of it, I feel hungry.

호접몽

천상에서 들려주는 매혹적인 목소리로

연애편지 실어 나르는 금빛 나빌 보았어요

꽃 눈 속 무한정으로 뒹구는 나는 예쁜, 꿈속이어요

The Dream of a Swallowtail Butterfly

A sound is heard from heaven;
  how enchanting the sound is!

A butterfly, shining like gold,
  is carrying a love letter.

In my dream, petals fall like snow
  and I'm rolling on and on.

햇빛 비상구

앞은 캄캄하고 뒤는 더욱 깜깜하여

방향을 틀어야 할 그런 때가 온다면

너에게 달려가고 싶다 젖 먹던 힘 다 모아서

Sunlight, the Emergency Exit

When it's dark in front of me
  and it's darker behind me

it may be time for me to change
  my direction, if possible.

In that case, I'd like to run to you
  with all the strength I can muster.

행복을 주는 사람

- 양훈이 형에게

이 땅에 착한 별 하나가 내려왔지

천상에서 가장 깨끗한 목소리 들려주며

다복함 통째로 내려주는 당신이라는 훈훈한 꽃

The Person Who Gives Happiness

– I dedicate this poem to Bro Yang-hun

A good star shot across the sky
  and came down to this land.

You've talked to us in the voice,
  the cleanest voice in heaven.

You must be a heartwarming flower
  that has made us feel blessed.

2부

뜨겁게 노래하거나 슬픔에 흠뻑 젖은 나날

Part 2

Days of Singing Passionately or Feeling Sad

상사화相思花

가슴에 데인 그런 사랑 한 번만 해봤으면

온몸이 오래 시려 지독하게 아픈 봄날에

저 대지大地 관절통 앓은 후 기지개 켤 붉은 꽃이여

Magic Lilies

Oh I wish I'd burn with love
  even though my heart aches.

My whole body has ached too long;
  though spring has come, I still feel pain.

Red flowers! You'll stretch from the ground
  that suffered from joint pain.

립스틱

가을도 아주 늦가을 한 그루 철쭉 꽃봉

그 봄날 화냥기가 여직 지지 않았나 보다

옷 벗은 느티나무 아래 발기物起를 돕는 저 강렬함

Lipstick

A flower bud of an azalea,
    though it's autumn, um, late autumn.

It still has the flirtation
    that women have in the spring.

The passion under the bare zelkova
    is helping to erect it.

치자꽃

섬 유월, 내 여자한테
치자꽃 향기가 났다

여섯 꽃잎 해풍에 살랑
바람개비로 떠도는 배

파도는 방아쇠를 당겼다
아, 꽃을 삼킨 흰 포말

Cape Jasmine Flower

My girl smelled like the floral scent
one day in June on the island.

Six petals swayed in the sea breeze;
each boat moved like whirling pin-wheels.

Oh perhaps the waves shot the gun.
White sea foam swallowed the petals.

어디만큼 오시나

보일 듯한 내 사랑아 어디만큼 오시나

계절이 또 슬쩍 지나 어둠이 속도 내는 길

로댕의 「생각하는 사람」처럼 말 안 해도 보일 사랑

Where Are You?

Oh, my love, where are you now?
  But I feel like I can see you.

A season passed before we know it;
  darkness falls pretty quickly.

Love is seen without any words,
  like 'The Thinker' by Rodin.

부부

강된장에 호박잎 쌈을 싸 먹는 초저녁

하루를 토닥이듯 홍련紅蓮으로 피는 말

"진하게 오래도록 살자"이 단단한 풀물 포옹

Husband and Wife

They eat rice wrapped in pumpkin leaves
  with soybean paste for early dinner.

As if hoping to cheer her up,
  he sweet-talks her, like a red lotus.

"Let's live long in a happy mood."
  The two hug with fresher hearts.

은근히

그 여자 샴푸 냄새가 문득 그리워지는

장미향 그 입술이 사무치게 그리워지는

통째로 탐하고 싶다, 푸른 가시 오월엔

Inwardly

Suddenly, I come to miss
  the good smell of her shampoo.

I intensely miss her lips
  that smell sweet like red roses.

Oh in May, I want to have them whole,
  when roses have bright green thorns.

지금, 대숲에는

대숲에 바람이 불면 파아란 해일海溢이 인다
태고의 북소리로 다가오는 정오正午여
영아의 울음소리 같은 알카리 음색이여.

지나간 자리마다 이끼 같은 정이 돋고
초록 물결 사이로 쏟아지는 햇살은
신神짚힌 댓잎소리로 물끄러미 비추고 있다

Now, in the Bamboo Grove

When it's windy in the bamboo grove,
  green bamboos sway like tidal waves.
Oh toward noon, the grove produces
  the loud sound of ancient drums.
Oh the sound that's good for our health,
  just like the cry of an infant.

Everywhere the wind passes,
  mosses grow with affection.
Oh the sun is blazing down
  through the green waves of bamboo leaves.
It's glinting off the bamboo leaves
  that are making curious sounds.

달개비

유리알처럼 투명한 늦가을 삼랑진역

철길 건너 '인간서점'*엔 거미들의 푸른 궁전

열차가 지날 때마다 파르르 몸을 떠는…

* 인간서점: 수십 년 전 폐업한 서점. 아직 철거되지 않고 걸려있는 간판만이
  옛 명성을 지키고 있음

Dayflower

Late Autumn, as clear as glass,
  I arrived at Samrangjin Station.

'Human Bookstore'* across the rail tracks;
  spiders made it their green palace.

Whenever rattling trains passed by,
  dayflowers trembled with fear.

---

* Human Bookstore: The bookstore was closed down decades ago,
  not yet demolished. Only the signboard keeps its old reputation.

질경이

흉터뿐인 그 이름도
한 번쯤 불러다오

별을 보고 칼을 받으며
퍼런 상처를 치유하였다

그 자리 부동의 자세로 서서
새 한 마리 꿈꾸었다

Plantain Herb

Even if it's covered with scars,
please call the name at least once.

Threatened with knives, looking at stars,
it kept healing its green wounds.

Standing still only in one place,
it has just dreamed of a bird.

장마 2
– 고추잠자리

내 젊은 날 꽃잎 진 자리 하염없이 몸이 젖는다
녹음綠陰에 날고 싶은 욕망을 짓누르기란
못다 푼 수학공식처럼 알 수 없는 미로여

굳게 잠긴 허공 열고, 붉은 태양 받아 들고
잿빛 상처 없는 동쪽으로 가고만 싶다
우주 끝 무지개다리 놓고 아다지오 아다지오

Rainy Season 2

－ A Red Dragonfly

Where petals fell in my youth,
  I kept getting wet in the rain.
Restraining the heart's desire
  to fly around among green trees.
Yes, it was a mysterious maze,
  like math problems I stopped solving.

Opening up the closed sky,
  and holding up the red sun,
I really want to go east,
  where there aren't any grey wounds.
At the end of the universe,
  I'll slowly put a rainbow bridge.

장마 3

– 매미의 허물

더 이상 울지 못하는 계절은 너무 슬프다

그 여름 불같은 말씀 연기처럼 사라진 언덕

청아한 코스모스 같은 마을운동회 한창이다

Rainy Season 3

- The Cast-off Skin of a Cicada

The cicada is so sad
in the season when it can't cry.

That summer, its fiery words
vanished like smoke from the hill.

In its place, pretty cosmos are swaying,
as if joining town sports events.

까마중이 익는 동안

잿빛 상처가 덧나는 저녁 답에

양철지붕 두들기며 국수 같은 비 내린다

젖동냥 나가신 아버지 오지 않아 속이 타고

While Sunberries Are Ripening

Gray-colored, my wound is getting
  worse and worse in the evening.

Rain is falling pitter-patter
  on the tin roof, like noodles fall.

I'm nervous, waiting for my dad
  who begs strangers for breast milk.

뜨거운 술

무덤가에 앉은 새가 엉엉 우는데 말입니다

봉분에 핀 할미꽃 주름 펴며 웃지 않겠습니까

이 봄날 새와 꽃이 나눈, 술이 참 뜨겁습니다

Hot Alcoholic Drink

A bird sits down, crying out loud,
  beside a grave, or burial mound.

A pasqueflower on the mound
  has a big smile with no wrinkles.

One spring day, the bird and the flowers
  shared the drink that's strong and hot.

뛰어가는 노을

낙동강 다리 난간에 걸터앉아 불을 듭니다
강 동네 아이들 음성 배어 있는 갈대숲은
뜨거운 꽃으로 피어 출렁이는 시간입니다

절망을 멀리했던 너와 나의 수채화가
홍시처럼 잘 익은 인정人情의 밥을 나누고
깔깔깔 새의 군무로 나란히 뛰어갑니다

Sunset Running

At sunset, I sit on the railing
  of the Nakdong River Bridge.
Children living near the river
  filled the reed field with their noises.
Now it's time for the swaying reeds
  to become red hot flowers.

You and I made our efforts
  to stay away from despair.
We shared meals, warming our hearts
  that resembled ripe persimmons.
Giggling, we ran side by side,
  like birds dancing together.

폭우

하늘 계신 어머니는 지상의 아들 보고 싶어

온종일 우레 치며 펑펑펑 우십니다

퍼내고 퍼내도 마르지 않는 황토빛 낙동강

Heavy Rain

My mother in heaven
  seems to miss her son on earth.

With thunder all day long,
  she's shedding tears, crying out loud.

Her tears flow into the Nakdong River
  that won't dry up, though I pump.

성구야

선불리 웃지 마라
장마의 날 있을 거다

함부로 젖지도 마라
우는 하늘 며칠이겠니

시인은 웃음도 울음도
절체절명에 쏟는 거야

Dear Seong-gu

Do not laugh all too soon.
There may be a rainy day.

Don't get wet in the rain.
How many days will it rain?

A poet has to laugh or cry
when dealing with life or death.

구체적 슬픔

나약한 그 남자의 속눈썹 처마 밑에는

칠월 장마 같은 슬픔이 살고 있었네

매미가 제 목소릴 묻은 건 천둥 키운 우기雨氣 때문

Definite Sorrow

The weak man had the eyelashes
  that were like eaves on a house.

Under them, there was sorrow
  that's like monsoon in July.

Cicadas had to stop chirping,
  as the monsoon brought loud thunders.

슬픔의 정석

둘이었다 혼자가 된 그 술집 모퉁이에

종일 비가 내린다, 양철 비가 추적추적

음악도 마음도 다 젖어 흐느끼는 골목집

A Mode of Sadness

We both were together;
   now I'm alone in a pub.

It's been raining all day long;
   the rain patters on the tin roof.

My heart cries along with music
   at the pub in the alley.

진짜 눈물

치밀어 오른 감정수憾情水는
심장 염분 백 퍼센트

사막의 모래바람이며
빙하 속 한 알 씨앗이며

묵직한 그 사람이 키워낸
정면승부의 붉은 뿌리

Real Tears

When tears burst forth from the heart,
their salt level is 100 percent.

The real tears are like sandstorms
or a small seed in a glacier.

Or red roots that a silent man grows
after his fight against something.

헐렁한 술의 시간

하느님의 눈물을 받아내는 강변 술집엔

독한 세상살이보다 술이 엄청 싱겁습니다

자존심 다 버린 술처럼 맹물과 섞여 종일 놉디다

Drinking Time with No Tension

God's teardrops fall down as rain
　　on the pub by the river.

Even though it's a tough world,
　　I'm drinking low alcohol drinks.

Such weak drinks, giving up all its pride,
　　are mixed with rain all day long.

3부

단풍이 물드는 자리에 바람과 별이 지나가고

Part 3

Where Foliage Turns Golden, Brown, and Red, Winds and Stars Pass By

홍옥

눈물에게 새빨간 심장이 있다는 걸

가을로 깊이 와서 비로소 알게 됐다

큰 한 입 베어 문 살점, 그 상처까지 맛나다니

Red Apple

People shed a lot of tears
    that may have a bright red heart.

Such a thought dawns upon me
    when late autumn is approaching.

I'm taking a big bite of the apple;
    the bite mark is also good.

억새꽃

오래전 잎잎들이 여린 살에 칼금 긋더니

눈썹이 세는 저물녘 솜꽃 가득 피운다

바람이 놀다 간 가을은 강물도 뜨겁게 진다

Silver Grass Flowers

So long ago, I got cut
   by a silver grass, sharp as a knife.

My eyebrows look white at dusk,
   when, like cotton, white flowers bloom.

In autumn, when the wind calms down,
   the river also turns red.

단풍 무덤

마지막 달력 한 장 남겨둔 밤이었다

바람 불어 스산하게 단풍잎 쌓이는 정원

벼랑 끝, 두 그림자가 바람에 흔들렸다

A Pile of Autumn Leaves

It was the night before turning
   the last page on the calendar.

Falling off trees in a bleak wind,
   red leaves piled up in the garden.

Two shadows were shaken by the wind
   at the edge of the cliff.

일몰

장밋빛 섹스가 시작되는 해질녘 강은

온종일 참아왔던 언어들이 눈뜨는 시간

태양의 굳센 근육으로 갈대밭을 물들인다

Sunset

At sunset, the river starts
   to make love with the rosy glow.

All day long, they didn't share words;
   now it's time for them to talk.

The strong glow of the setting sun
   makes a reed field tinged with red.

모과향

검버섯 가득한 저 늙은 여배우의 몸

진갈색 딱딱한 상처 그대 본 일 있는가

들국菊이 천지사방 번져 갈 때 몸을 씻는 가을 편지

The Scent of Quince Fruit

The fruit's covered with age spots
　like the body of an old actress.

Have you seen dark brown bruises
　on the surface of the hard fruit?

The fruit is like a letter from autumn
　when camomile spreads here and there.

감잎 단풍

첫서리가 새빨간 감잎에 앉았습니다

쭈글쭈글한 가슴으로 달에게 젖을 물린

대봉시 감분 같은 어머니, 단풍 한 잎이 눈물입니다

Autumn-colored Persimmon Leaves

Oh the first frost of the season
  on the red leaves of persimmon trees.

Soft persimmons make me think
  Mom gives the moon her wrinkled breast.

Oh my mom who's like a dried persimmon;
  each autumn leaf is my teardrops.

살구나무죽비

무쇠 같은 하루가 노을에 닿는 시간
시퍼런 몸에 감춰진 찌든 먼지 털어낸다
속 비운 살구나무죽비, 내 등에서 꽃 핀다

꽉 막힌 혈전들이 녹아내리는 몸속 행간
천 년 전 바람 냄새 스멀스멀 배어들면
그 봄을 기억하는 살구, 몸의 터널 환하다

The Apricot Wood Stick

Tough as iron, I get through a day
  and then see the glow of sunset.
I shake off the dust hidden
  in my body that looks bruised.
When I use the hollow stick for health,
  flowers seem to bloom on my back,

The stick helps dissolve blood clots
  that block blood flow in my body.
Oh I smell the wind that blew
  a thousand years ago.
Apricots, remembering the spring,
  also help blood flow in my body.

일상

고장 난 시계가 눈 잠깐 붙이는데

하루의 수리공이 문을 자꾸 두드린다

저만치 밀려간 파도, 거품 물고 다시 오는

Daily Routine

The clock is out of order,
  wanting to sleep for a moment.

However, its repairman
  is knocking at my door.

It's common; sea waves too roll out
  and come again with sea foam.

달의 이미지

강 문장文章을 읽으며 난다
청둥오리 일가족

달의 몸에 밑줄 긋고
강물에겐 물음표 하나

모래 위 적어놓은 생의 답
웃으며 읽는 달이 두 개

The Image of the Moon

A family of mallard ducks
read the river, while they're flying.

They underline the bright moon
with one question mark on the river.

The answer to life written on the sand;
two moons read it with a smile.

해질녘 강가에 앉아

미루나무 가지 꺾어 회초리 만들었습니다
저 먼 길 끝, 아버지께서 내 종아리 내리치듯이
오늘은 강가에 나와 앉아, 강물 세게 내리칩니다

강물 금세 피멍 같은 노을로 물들고
야생 꽃들 소리 내어 나 대신 흠씬 웁니다
두 눈이 퉁퉁 부은 낙동강 종이배 띄워놓고

Sitting by the River at Sunset

I cut a branch from a poplar tree
   and made a stick to hit something.
Just like my dad, who passed away,
   had hit me in the calf,
I'm hitting the flowing river hard
   by the river now today.

Like getting bruised, the river
   is colored with sunset soon.
Imagining wild flowers
   cry out loud instead of me.
I'm floating, on the Nakdong River,
   a paper boat with swollen eyes.

가을 탁발托鉢

벼랑 끝 엉켜 있는 주홍 노을 한 장이

너무 빠른 주검들을 따듯이 덮어주듯

내 등을 토닥여줍니다 한 바가지 단풍 물로

Asking for Autumn

The red glow of the sunset
  on the edge of a cliff.

The glow looks like it's covering
  the poor things that died too early.

Moreover, it's patting me on the back
  with autumn tints in abundance.

각북角北에 앉아 있다

각북에 가지 않고 각북에 앉아 있다
열두 나절 서성이는 시집 속 뿔의 마을
복사꽃 지고 난 가지 끝 유월 뻐꾸기 피어난다

꽉 막힌 동맥과 터져버린 정맥을 위해
정자나무 품속으로 내 심장이 날아가고
청나비 푸른 그늘을 이고 덩실덩실 단풍 든다

Sitting in Gakbuk Town

I seem to sit in Gakbuk Town,
  though I don't go to the town.
The horn-like town in my book of poems;
  for twelve days, I've hung around there.
Peach blossoms have all fallen off;
  in June cuckoos sit on the branch.

For the treatment of broken veins
  as well as clogged arteries,
my mind flies, in a hurry,
  to a shade tree in the town.
A young kid dancing under the green shade;
  the cheeks flush with excitement.

옻단풍

발가벗은 겨울이
다시 불을 놓은 날

옻순 몰래 먹은 여자
삼백일 품은 기도처럼

늦가을, 가려움 한 잎이
새빨갛게 물듭니다

A Lacquer Tree With Fall Foliage

In winter, trees shed their clothes,
but I see flames rising again.

A girl praying for 300 days
secretly ate lacquer tree shoots.

Like late fall, her body has got red,
as she's suffered severe itching.

시詩를 업은 항아리

네 몸에 새겨놓은
달빛 문장 은은하다

천길 불구덩이도
견뎌낸 애절한 사랑

온 우주 어르고 달랜 귀얄문
둥개둥개 업어 키운다

A Ceramic Pot with a Poem on It

The words inscribed on the body
look subtle in the moonlight.

The pot survived in the hot kiln
with ardent love for the poem.

The brush marks, soothing the universe,
help the love grow on the pot.

막차 떠난 후 불시착

영동 산간에 유례없는 폭설이 내렸다

남도 끝 양지쪽엔 구절초 개나리 웃네

가을은 고속열차로 떠났네 개찰 안 한 봄이네

Crash Landing After the Last Train Left

Heavy snow fell beyond records
　　on the mountains of Yeongdong Area.

But in the warmth of Southern regions,
　　forsythias smile with wild daisies.

Autumn left on a high-speed train.
　　With tickets unchecked, spring has come.

잠시, 노을에 젖다

속이 까만 한 사내가
달아공원* 일몰을 본다

번개탄 하나 둘 셋 넷…
마지막까지 말없이 잠든,

바다는 무연고의 무덤
조문 없어 울 일도 없는

*달아공원: 통영을 대표하는 명소 중 하나

Basking in the Glow of Sunset for a While

So frustrated, a man facing
the sunset at Dal-a Park.

One, two, three, four charcoal briquettes;
leaving no words, he ended up dead.

The sea is a grave with no relatives,
no mourners, no need to cry.

* Dal-a Park: one of the most famous attractions in Tongyeong City

불균형의 가을

단풍 든 네 가을의 오른쪽은 무척 환하다

벌레 먹은 나의 왼쪽은 어둠이 매우 깊다

무작정 흔들고 가는 이 스산한 편두통

Unbalanced Autumn

With the glow of autumn leaves,
　the right side is very bright.

But alas, eaten by bugs,
　my left side is very dark.

Suffering from severe migraine
　I feel shaken to the core.

늙은 우산

가슴을 다 적셔야만 안 보이던 당신이 오지

철없는 작달비 응석, 말없이 받아내던

당신은 무사하신가요? 세파에 꺾여 녹슨 뼈대여

Old Umbrella

Invisible! But you are seen
  when I get soaked to my chest.

You've been willing to pamper
  heavy rains without complaints.

Are you fine? Oh no, your rusty frame;
  you have suffered from hardships.

관념

몽유병 환자였네 쓰잘머리 없는 헛꿈만 차서

한 하늘 한 생이 온통, 청보랏빛 추상抽象이네

먹어도 배를 못 불린 서정과 현실 사이

Notion

Filling my head with useless dreams,
  I have been a sleepwalker.

Both the sky and my whole life
  are blue purple in the abstract.

Oh feeling differs from reality;
  though I eat a lot, I feel hungry.

4부

얼음의 날을 견디며 간절히 올리는 청동거울 시문詩文

Part 4

Hoping My Poems Will Shine Long like a Bronze Mirror
by Enduring Tough Days

대竹

엄동에 얼음의 날도 넉넉히 넘어서서

그대 그 도도함 칼날 같은 푸른 기상은

오로지 한 길을 비추시는 아버지의 댓잎 눈빛

Bamboo

Oh bamboo, you overcame
   the freezing cold of winter.

Positively glowing with pride,
   you're showing a sharp spirit.

My father pursued only one way;
   his eyes looked like bamboo leaves.

먹

내 굳은 피 묽게 갈아 세상을 세우리라

한 획으로 넘쳐나는 견고한 말씀의 나라

죽어도 죽지 않을 혼이여! 그 어둠을 쉬게 하라

Calligraphy Ink Stick

I will grind my congealed blood
   to make the world stand up straight.

Carefully with each stroke,
   I will make the world of words.

Oh spirit that won't disappear after death!
   Let the darkness rest in peace.

불두화

해年를 지날 때마다
업業 한 겹 더 쌓인다

천둥 같은 북소리가
심장을 찢고 하혈하는 밤

촛농이 법당 가득 메워도
열리지 않는 마음꽃

Snowball Flower

Whenever each year goes by,
karma piles up one by one.

The temple drum sounds like thunder;
my heart seems torn, bleeding at night.

The flower won't open its heart,
though candle drips may fill the shrine.

조장鳥葬

불온한 생각들이 지켜온 몸 버리려 하네

살과 가죽은 뜯어 굶주린 새 먹이로 주고

허공에 난蘭을 치겠네 깨끗해진 영혼으로

Sky Burial

I have lived, full of wrong thoughts.
  Please leave my corpse exposed outside.

My flesh and skin will be devoured
  by hungry birds, namely vultures.

Feeling cleansed, my soul will fly up,
  drawing orchids in the air.

흉터

고여 있는 눈물은 상처가 매우 깊다

실로도 꿰맬 수 없는 문드러진 자국처럼

검정피 온몸에 번져 행간마다 동풍動風이 불어

Scar

Tears don't fall from my eyes,
  as I feel deeply wounded.

The deep wound can't be sewn up,
  though threads are used to suture it.

Black blood spreads all through my body,
  so I feel cramped all over.

일기

등을 켠 사멸의 하루
녹는 눈처럼 운다고

채우지 못한 네 빈자리
어쩌겠느냐 어쩌겠느냐

붓 끝에 잠시 멈춘 시간
뜨겁게 필 내일인 걸

Diary

At nightfall with a lamp on
I'm weeping like melting snow.

I haven't yet filled the empty space.
What should I do? What should I do?

Let me stop moving the brush, though;
tomorrow will surely come.

가랑잎 환청

초겨울 지는 잎들
가랑가랑 들리는 소리

봄새 같은 어머니는
산무덤쯤 꽃 피웠네

심골心骨에 함박눈 내려
손톱이 긁는 저 시린 말

Fallen Leaves Rustling

Fallen leaves of early winter
are making a rustling sound.

My mother who's like a spring bird;
there are flowers around her grave.

Soothing me, it's snowing in large flakes;
fallen leaves scratch their fingernails.

지우개밥

울컥 치밀어 오른 가난의 여백들이

헛헛한 뱃속 채우려고 한 술의 밥 떠 넣었네

배설한 저 기형의 똥을 울며 먹네 시인은

Eraser Debris

Something burst inside me;
  I am choked with poverty.

To appease my hunger,
  I just eat a spoonful of rice.

Deformed wastes left after erasing
  I eat in tears, as I'm a poet.

아버지의 포옹

가슴엔 늘 날끼이 선, 말만 품은 줄 알았네

그 눈빛도 가시로만 돋은 줄 알았었네

꿈에서 슬쩍 안으며 웃는, 그윽한 눈빛 내 아버지

Father's Embrace

I just thought my father had
  only sharp words in his heart.

And I thought he had the gaze
  that's piercing just like a thorn.

But smiling with a loving gaze,
  he hugs me in my dream.

고사목

지리산 법계사 근처
산 등허리 한입 물고

온몸으로 비를 맞는
까마귀 몇 마리

울지도 날지도 못해
우두커니 슬프다

Dead Tree

I see the tree near Beopgye Temple
on the ridge of Mount Jiri.

A few crows are sitting
on the branches in the rain.

Oh alas! They are motionless,
neither cawing nor flying off.

어떤 동백 시집

맹물 같은 시집 한 권이
처녀성을 열었습니다

천 일 참다 한 번 준 마음
절정의 값 단돈 만 원에

눈밭 위 모가지째 낭자한
핏빛 핏빛 절규여!

A Poetry Book, Just like a Camellia Flower

A collection of my poems
just came out like a virgin.

A thousand days of endurance;
the book is priced at ten dollars.

My goodness, I'm like the fallen flower
that looks bloody on the snow.

다듬어진다는 것

세상이 얼마만큼
많은 모로 널브러졌으면

저리도 끊임없이
반복 재생만 되뇌나

예쁘게 다듬어진다는 건
원형을 깨는 슬픈 정점頂點

Getting Better

How messy is the world?
Has it been in disarray?

Why on earth does the world keep
constantly changing like that?

So sadly, to make something better,
original forms should be broken.

11월

서녘의 가을이 아주 깊숙이 들어왔다

영식이 집 감나무에 매달린 저 웃음 한 통

지금은, 가슴 저미도록 푸른 별로 반짝인다

November

The sunset glows in the west;
   it's approaching late autumn.

The persimmon tree in Yeongsik's house
   looked cheerful with red persimmons.

Memories of those far-off days;
   now they're twinkling as blue stars.

봉인

불을 켜지 말아요
비 오고 눈 내려도

마른 꽃이 다시 핀대도
천 년쯤 가둘 이 울음 박물博物

신이여 누설 말아요
햇볕 드는 그날까지

Sealing

Please don't turn the light on,
even though it rains or snows.

Lock up this cry for a thousand years,
though dried flowers may bloom again.

Oh, dear god, do not let it out
until the sun shines on it.

슬픈 달관達觀

심장에 옹이가 박혀
타다 만 옹이가 박혀

눈물의 혈소판까지
다 태운 강물처럼

실성한 내 그림자는
독학獨學의 노을입니다

Sad Transcendence

There's sadness deep in my heart;
it burned a bit, leaving a grudge.

My tears of blood kept running down,
just as if a river flows.

My shadow that looks unusual;
it's the result from self-study.

청동거울 시문詩文

마음이란 장작불로 영혼을 태운 청동의 시

수천 번 되불러도 싫증나지 않을 노래

천국서 발굴된다면 그 천국이 환하겠네

My Poetry, a Bronze Mirror

With all my soul, I write poems
   that will last quite long like bronze.

The poems won't wear us down,
   though they're recited thousands of times.

If poems are written in heaven,
   the heaven will get bright.

나뭇잎 장례식

깊고 깊은 잠 속에서 환영幻影을 읽는다

꽃상여 앞소리에 갈잎 한 장 떨어진다

아버지 그 강직함이 일순간 무너지는 찰나 …

Funeral by a Leaf

While I am in a deep sleep,
　I see something I imagine.

An autumn leaf falls with the dirge
　by the leader of pallbearers.

Ah alas, my dad's uprightness
　disappears at that moment.

어머니라는 이름과 아버지라는 이름 사이,
내 이름이 참으로 따뜻하게 피어 있었음을 …

갓길에 핀 풋 찔레꽃도
울음 매우 따뜻했네

가슴을 다 도려 내놓고
빛 한 줌 들이기까지

우주를 오래 에돌아 와서
참회 눈물로 벙그네

How Sweet My Name Was Between Mom and Dad

Oh wild roses beside the road;
even their tears were so warm.

Having my heart wide open,
I let in a handful of light.

Now I shed tears of repentance,
as I wandered around the world.

번역자 우형숙

현재 국제PEN 한국본부 번역위원장, 국제계관시인연합회 한국본부 번역위원으로 활동 중. 시조시인이고 영문학박사(시번역 전공)이며 모교인 숙명여자대학교(25년)와 세종대학교(5년)(겸임교수)에서 영문학 및 번역 강의 후 은퇴.

시조시인으로서 3권의 시조집을 출간하였으며, 번역가로서 한국의 시집 및 시조집 20여 권을 영어로 번역. 한국시조문학번역상과 국제PEN한국본부로부터 PEN번역문학상을 수상한 바 있음.

About the Translator Woo Hyeong-sook

Woo Hyeong-sook now serves as the head of the translation committee of International PEN - Korean Center. She is also on the translation committee of the United Poets Laureate International - Korean Center. With a doctorate in English literature(major: poetry translation), she taught English literature and translation at her alma mater, Sookmyung Women's University for 25 years and Sejong University for 5 years as an adjunct professor.

As a sijo poet, she has published three collections of her sijo poems. As a translator, she has translated over 20 collections of Korean poems and sijo poems into English. She received the Korean Sijo Translation Award and the PEN Translation Award from International PEN-Korean Center.